Gilda and Friends

Lucky

An orphan leopard
cub who has the
worst luck

Pepin

A persistent
penguin who loves
his family

Marvin

A silly little
marmoset who is
afraid of heights

Ernest

A young elephant who is
very afraid of mice

Gilda

A friendly giraffe who
loves melons and parties

Zander

A caring,
wise zebra who looks
out for his friends

Leonardo

An adventurous little
lion cub who likes to
go exploring

Papaya

A lovable panda who
eats a lot of bamboo

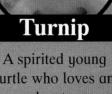

Turnip

A spirited young
turtle who loves an
adventure

We hope you enjoy the many adventures of Gilda and Friends. Our goal was to maintain the spirit of the original French-language story while adapting it to the Picture Window Books' format. Thank you to the original publisher, author, and illustrator for allowing Picture Window Books to make this series available to a new audience.

Editor: Jacqueline A. Wolfe
Page Production: Tracy Kaehler
Creative Director: Keith Griffin
Editorial Director: Carol Jones
Managing Editor: Catherine Neitge

First American edition published in 2006 by
Picture Window Books
5115 Excelsior Boulevard
Suite 232
Minneapolis, MN 55416
877-845-8392
www.picturewindowbooks.com

First published in Canada in 2000 by
Les éditions Héritage inc.
300 Arran Street, Saint Lambert
Quebec, Canada J4R 1K5

Printed in the United States of America.

Library of Congress Cataloging-in-Publication Data
Papineau, Lucie.
Gilda the giraffe and Papaya the panda / by Lucie Papineau ; illustrated by Marisol Sarrazin.
p. cm. "Gilda the giraffe."
Summary: Papaya the panda is allergic to raindrops and when he gets caught in a downpour and begins to shrink, he searches desperately for safety to avoid disappearing altogether.
ISBN 1-4048-1293-8 (hardcover)
[1. Pandas—Fiction. 2. Animals—Fiction. 3. Size—Fiction.] I. Sarrazin, Marisol, 1965—ill. II. Title.
PZ7.P2115Gil 2005
[E]—dc22   2005011346

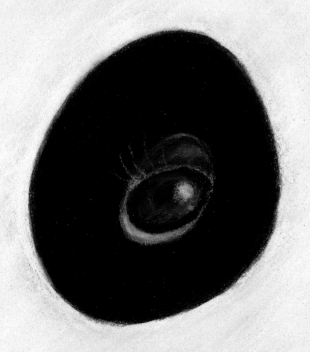
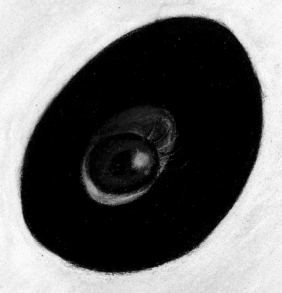

Gilda the Giraffe

and

Papaya the Panda

by Lucie Papineau
illustrated by Marisol Sarrazin
story adapted by Michael Dahl

PICTURE WINDOW BOOKS
Minneapolis, Minnesota

The magical jungle, where Gilda the giraffe and her friends live, is famous for bright blue skies and warm sunshine.

But one day, a little cloud sailed into the sky. A very dark, little cloud.

"It looks like rain," said Gilda. "We should look for shelter. But where is Papaya?" she wondered. "We'd better find him to warn him!"

The orangutan and the crocodile just shrugged. They didn't know where Papaya was either.

Deep in the bamboo forest, far from his three friends, Papaya the panda chewed on some tasty bamboo.

He was so busy enjoying the delicious treat, he didn't see the dark cloud growing bigger and bigger.

6

PLINK! A raindrop fell on a leafy bush.

PLUNK! A second drop fell on a nearby rock.

PLONK! A third drop fell on Papaya's head.

7

"Oh, no!" cried Papaya. The bamboo surrounding him grew taller and taller. The tiny bugs at his feet grew larger and larger.

"I'm shrinking!" shouted Papaya.

Soon, Papaya was no bigger than a mouse.

The tiny panda ran as fast as his tiny feet could carry him. He went searching for his friends. He was sure they would be able to help him.

Just then a booming voice roared overhead. **"Papayaaaaa!"**

It was Papaya's friend the orangutan.

"Over here," cried Papaya. But his tiny voice could not be heard above the thunder of the storm.

The orangutan bounded through the forest, searching for his friend. In a few more steps, his foot would crush the tiny panda.

"LOOK OUT!" yelled Papaya. But his friend could not hear him.

The frightened panda dashed to safety. He curled into a furry ball and went plunging down a steep slope.

11

SPLASH!

The panda fell into a small stream. But to little Papaya, the stream looked more like a gigantic river.

"Help! Help!" shouted Papaya.

13

14

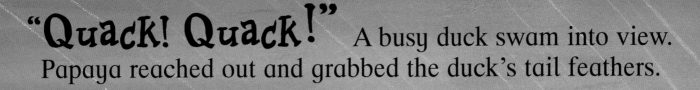

"Quack! Quack!" A busy duck swam into view. Papaya reached out and grabbed the duck's tail feathers.

"Safe at last," sighed Papaya.

Then the panda saw a monstrous mouth heading straight for him. It was his friend the crocodile calling out, "Papaya! Papaya!"

To the little panda, the toothy smile looked like a deadly trap!

Suddenly, the duck flew into the air, right above the jaws of the crocodile.

"Thank goodness!" Papaya said to himself. "I'm out of danger."

But Papaya was tossed about in the wind as the duck flew through the jungle. It was all he could do to hold on to the duck's tail feathers.

"This is worse than the river," said Papaya. Then a crash of lightning startled the duck so much he jerked and little Papaya lost his grip.

18

Swirling toward the ground, Papaya was
scared. He landed with a huge thump,
right on Gilda's head!

"Thank goodness! It's Gilda!" cried
Papaya. "She'll help me!"

19

But Papaya was so small, Gilda thought a bug had landed between her ears.

"That tickles," said Gilda.

And with a toss of her head, the giraffe sent her little friend sliding down her back like a bobsled down a mountain slope.

Papaya landed with a plop among soft, wet leaves on the ground of the jungle. "No one will find me now!" he wailed.

"Why, that bug looks just like a panda," came a nearby voice.

"I AM a panda!" yelled Papaya.

A smiling turtle crawled out of the dripping flowers. "But real pandas are much bigger than you," she said.

"I'm allergic to raindrops," said Papaya. "They are making me shrink."

"Oh, my!" the turtle said. "You must be very frightened. Why don't you crawl inside my shell and dry off? I was just going out for a nice shower anyway."

23

Inside the turtle's shell, Papaya felt safe at last.

Soon, the rain stopped. The sun peeked out from behind the dark cloud. The warm air dried Papaya's wet fur.

But, when he woke up, Papaya felt very strange. He could hardly breathe!

Now that his fur was dry, Papaya had grown back to his normal size. But he was still stuck inside the turtle's shell!

"It's too tight!" he wheezed.

"Papaya!" cried Gilda. "Where have you been? We've looked everywhere for you! We were so worried you'd shrink from the raindrops and get hurt!"

The three friends were so happy that they each gave Papaya a great, big hug.

SSssSsssss! Papaya shrank again, slipping out of the shell like a punctured balloon.

"The rain on your coats saved me!" cried the once again tiny Papaya. "The rainwater made me shrink again, and I slipped right out of the shell."

In a little while, Papaya
was dry again and back to
his regular size.

To show his gratitude for his
friends' help, he hosted a
special party and served the
tastiest bamboo he could find.

"No matter what size I am,"
said Papaya, "my friends
always make me feel
10 feet tall!"

Fun facts about Gilda's friends ...

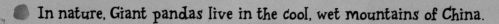

- In nature, Giant pandas live in the cool, wet mountains of China.

- Panda males grow to be about 6 feet (2 meters) tall.

- Pandas eat 15 different kinds of bamboo. They spend about 14 hours a day eating and have been recorded to eat up to 84 pounds (38 kilograms) of bamboo in a day.

- Pandas have a special, muscular lining in their stomachs. The lining protects the panda from the tough, sharp pieces of chewed up bamboo.

- Pandas have thick, oily, waterproof fur. The fur keeps rainwater from reaching their skin.

- Pandas are one of the few kinds of bears that do not hibernate.

Go on more adventures with Gilda the Giraffe:

Gilda the Giraffe and Leonardo the Lion Cub
Gilda the Giraffe and Lucky the Leopard
Gilda the Giraffe and Marvin the Marmoset
Gilda the Giraffe and Pepin the Penguin
No More Melons for Gilda the Giraffe
No Spots for Gilda the Giraffe!

On the Web

FactHound offers a safe, fun way to find Internet sites related to this book. All of the sites on FactHound have been researched by our staff.

Here's how:

1. Visit www.facthound.com

2. Type in this special code for age-appropriate sites: 1404812938

3. Click on the FETCH IT button.

Your trusty FactHound will fetch the best sites for you!

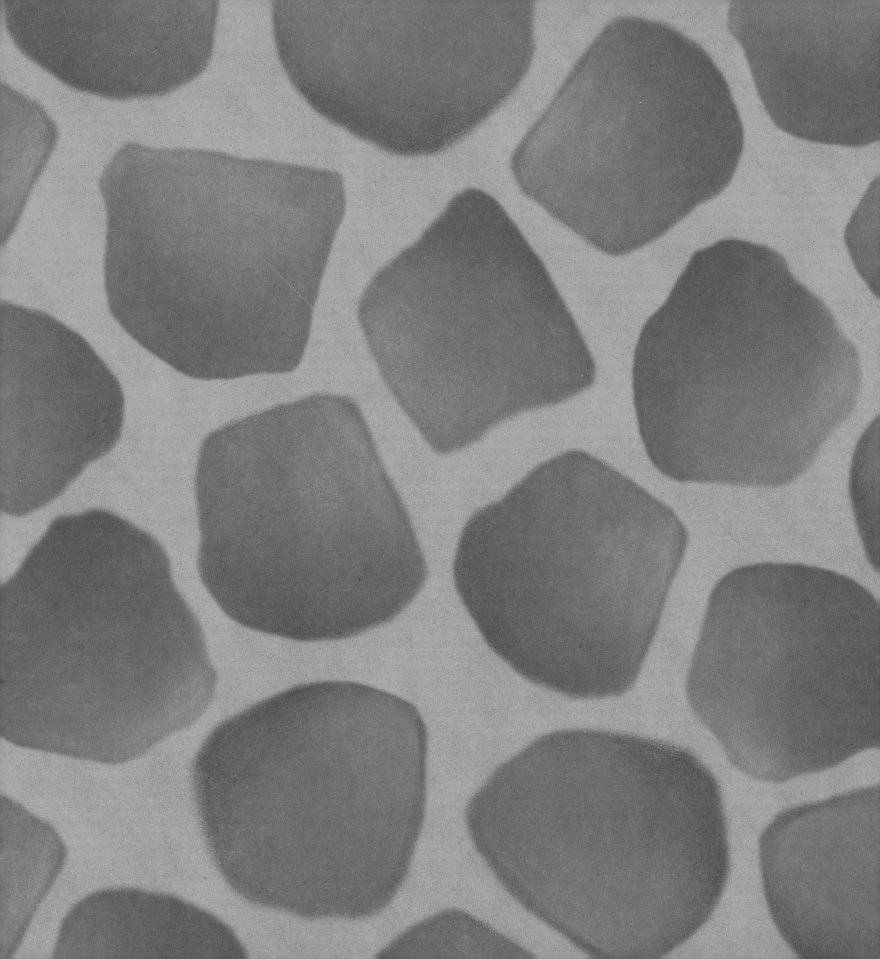